The
Bloomsbury
Nursery
Treasury

This book is for Sasha Pierina
P.B.

This book is for Sally,
Kenny, Lachlan & Jock
E.T.

Bloomsbury Publishing, London, Berlin and New York

First published in Great Britain in September 2010 by Bloomsbury Publishing Plc
36 Soho Square, London, W1D 3QY

A CIP catalogue record of this book is available from the British Library

ISBN 978 0 7475 9747 6

Printed in China by C&C Offset Printing Co Ltd, Shenzhen, Guangdong

1 3 5 7 9 10 8 6 4 2

FSC
Mixed Sources
Product group from well-managed
forests and other controlled sources
Cert no. SCS-COC-003548
www.fsc.org
© 1996 Forest Stewardship Council

www.bloomsbury.com/childrens

The
Bloomsbury
Nursery
Treasury

Patricia Borlenghi

ILLUSTRATED BY
Eleanor Taylor

BLOOMSBURY

LONDON BERLIN NEW YORK

Contents

Little Red Riding Hood

Once upon a time, there was a little girl who lived in a tiny village surrounded by woods. She was a sweet little girl and all the people in the village were very fond of her. She was doted on by her parents and she was a special favourite of her grandmother. This caring old lady had made her an unusual red hood, rather like a riding hood, and it made her look so cute that everybody called her Little Red Riding Hood.

One day, her mother made a fruit pie and said to her daughter, 'My darling, please go and see how your grandmother is. She hasn't been at all well and I'd like you to find out if she's any better. This pie should cheer her up.'

Little Red Riding Hood immediately set out to visit her grandmother, who lived in the next village. She had to walk through the wood to reach her grandmother's house. As she was walking through the lonely wood, she met a wolf.

The wolf was a sly old thing and he would have loved to eat the little girl for his dinner. But just now he didn't dare, because there were woodcutters nearby chopping down some tall trees. Instead the cunning wolf asked her where she was going.

The little girl was so innocent that she didn't realise how dangerous it was to stop and talk to a strange wolf, so she replied, 'I'm going to see my grandmother. I'm taking her a fruit pie that Mummy made for her.'

'Does she live near here?' asked the wolf.

'Oh, yes,' said Little Red Riding Hood, 'just at the end of this wood, at the first house in the next village.'

'Well,' said the wolf, 'I'll go and see her too. I know! You go that way and I'll go this way, and we'll see who gets there quickest.'

The wolf, who knew a short cut, ran as fast as he could. The little girl, who had taken the long, winding route, stopped every once in a while to gather nuts or wild flowers, and to chase the beautiful butterflies she saw fluttering around.

The wolf soon arrived at the grandmother's house. He knocked on the door.

'Who's there?' the grandmother asked in a frail voice.

'Your granddaughter, Little Red Riding Hood,' the wolf said, trying rather unsuccessfully to make his voice higher, like a little girl's. 'I've brought you a lovely fruit pie that Mummy made.'

The dear old lady, who was still in bed, cried out, 'Raise the latch and the door will open.'

The wolf lifted the latch and the door opened. He rushed to the old grandmother and ate her all up as fast as he could. He was ravenously hungry as he hadn't eaten anything for three days.

After that, the wolf shut the door, got into the grandmother's bed and waited for Little Red Riding Hood to arrive. When she reached the house, she knocked at the door.

'Who's there?' the wolf asked gruffly.

When Little Red Riding Hood first heard the wolf's voice, she was afraid. But she thought it was her grandmother's bad cold that made her voice sound hoarse, so she replied, 'It's your granddaughter, Little Red Riding Hood. I've brought you a lovely fruit pie that Mummy made.'

Trying to soften his voice as much as he could, the wolf cried out to her, 'Lift the latch and the door will open.'

Little Red Riding Hood did as she was told and the door opened.

When she came inside, the wolf hid himself under the bedclothes and said, 'Put the fruit pie on the table and come and sit on the bed by me.'

So Little Red Riding Hood took off her red hood and sat on the bed. The wolf slowly came out from under the bedclothes. Little Red Riding Hood was so surprised to see how peculiar her grandmother looked in her nightclothes that she let out a gasp.

'Oh, Grandmother, what **big arms** you've got!'

'All the better to hug you with, my pretty one,' the wolf replied.

'Oh, Grandmother, what **big ears** you've got!'

'All the better to hear you with, my little one.'

'Oh, Grandmother, what **big eyes** you've got!'

'All the better to see you with, my sweetie-pie.'

'Oh, Grandmother, what **big teeth** you've got!'

'All the better to eat you with!'

And with that the wicked wolf grabbed Little Red Riding Hood and ate her all up.

Henny Penny

One day, Henny Penny was eating corn in the farmyard when an acorn from the oak tree hit her on the head.

'Goodness gracious me!' said Henny Penny. **'The sky is falling in!** I must go and tell the king.'

So she went along and she went along and she went along, until she met Cocky Locky.

'Where are you going, Henny Penny?' asked Cocky Locky.

'Oh, I'm going to tell the king **the sky is falling in**,' said Henny Penny.

'May I come with you?' asked Cocky Locky.

'Of course,' said Henny Penny.

So Henny Penny and Cocky Locky went to tell the king the sky was falling in.

They went along and they went along and they went along, until they met Ducky Lucky.

'Where are you going, Henny Penny and Cocky Locky?' asked Ducky Lucky.

'Oh, we're going to tell the king **the sky is**

falling in,'
said Henny Penny
and Cocky Locky.

'May I come with
you?' asked Ducky Lucky.

'Of course,' said Henny Penny
and Cocky Locky.

So Henny Penny, Cocky Locky and Ducky Lucky
went to tell the king the sky was falling in.

They went along and they went along and they
went along, until they met Goosey Poosey.

'Where are you going, Henny Penny, Cocky Locky
and Ducky Lucky?' asked Goosey Poosey.

'Oh, we're going to tell the king **the sky is
falling in**,' said Henny Penny, Cocky Locky and
Ducky Lucky.

'May I come with you?' asked
Goosey Poosey.

'Of course,' said Henny Penny, Cocky Locky and Ducky Lucky.

So Henny Penny, Cocky Locky, Ducky Lucky and Goosey Poosey went to tell the king the sky was falling in.

They went along and they went along and they went along, until they met Turkey Lurkey.

'Where are you going, Henny Penny, Cocky Locky, Ducky Lucky and Goosey Poosey?' asked Turkey Lurkey.

'Oh, we're going to tell the king **the sky is falling in**,' said Henny Penny, Cocky Locky, Ducky Lucky and Goosey Poosey.

'May I come with you, Henny Penny, Cocky Locky, Ducky Lucky and Goosey Poosey?' asked Turkey Lurkey.

'Why, of course you can, Turkey Lurkey,' said Henny Penny, Cocky Locky, Ducky Lucky and Goosey Poosey.

So Henny Penny, Cocky Locky, Ducky Lucky, Goosey Poosey and Turkey Lurkey all went to tell the king the sky was falling in.

They went along and they went along and they went along, until they met Foxy Woxy.

'Where are you going, Henny Penny, Cocky Locky, Ducky Lucky, Goosey Poosey and Turkey Lurkey?' asked Foxy Woxy.

'We're going to tell the king **the sky is falling in**,' said Henny Penny, Cocky Locky, Ducky Lucky, Goosey Poosey and Turkey Lurkey.

'But this isn't the way to see the king, Henny Penny, Cocky Locky, Ducky Lucky, Goosey Poosey and Turkey Lurkey,' said Foxy Woxy. 'I know the right way. Shall I show you?'

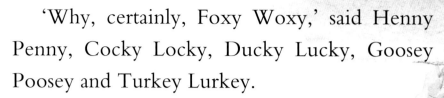

'Why, certainly, Foxy Woxy,' said Henny Penny, Cocky Locky, Ducky Lucky, Goosey Poosey and Turkey Lurkey.

So Henny Penny, Cocky Locky, Ducky Lucky, Goosey Poosey, Turkey Lurkey and Foxy Woxy all went to tell the king the sky was falling in.

They went along and they went along and they went along, until they came to a narrow, dark hole. Little did they know that this was the entrance to Foxy Woxy's den.

But Foxy Woxy said, 'This is the short cut to the king's palace – you'll soon reach it if you follow me. I'll go in first and then you should follow me, Henny Penny, Cocky Locky, Ducky Lucky, Goosey Poosey and Turkey Lurkey.'

'Of course,' said Henny Penny, Cocky Locky, Ducky Lucky, Goosey Poosey and Turkey Lurkey.

So Foxy Woxy went into his den and waited for Henny Penny, Cocky Locky, Ducky Lucky, Goosey Poosey and Turkey Lurkey.

Turkey Lurkey was the first to go through the narrow, dark hole into the den. He hadn't got far when . . . **Snap!** Foxy Woxy bit off Turkey Lurkey's head and threw him down.

Then Goosey Poosey went in and . . . **Snap!** Off came her head too, and Goosey Poosey was thrown beside Turkey Lurkey.

Then Ducky Lucky waddled through and . . . **Snap!** Her head was bitten off, and Ducky Lucky was thrown beside Turkey Lurkey and Goosey Poosey.

Then Cocky Locky strutted down into the den when . . . **Snap!** Off came his head, and Cocky Locky was thrown beside Turkey Lurkey, Goosey Poosey and Ducky Lucky.

But Foxy Woxy had to bite Cocky Locky twice as the first bite wasn't enough to kill him. After the first bite, Cocky Locky managed to call out to Henny Penny, 'Don't come down here, Henny Penny, or Foxy Woxy will kill you dead.'

So Henny Penny turned round and ran and ran and ran until she reached the farmyard, and she never told the king the sky was falling in.

The Three
Little Pigs

Once upon a time, there was a mother pig with three little pigs that she could not afford to keep. So she sent them away to make their own homes.

The first little pig went off and met a man with a bundle of straw. He said to him, 'Please, mister, give me that straw so I can build myself a house with it.'

The man agreed and the little pig built a house out of straw.

Not long after, along came a wolf.

He knocked at the door and said, 'Little pig, little pig, let me come in.'

The little pig answered, 'No, no, not by the hair of my chinny chin chin.'

The wolf replied, 'Then I'll **huff** and I'll **puff**, and I'll blow your house down.'

So he **huffed** and he **puffed**, and he blew the house down.

The second little pig met a man with a bundle of sticks. He said to him, 'Please, mister, give me those sticks so I can build a house.'

The man agreed and the little pig built his house out of sticks.

Then along came the wolf, who said, 'Little pig, little pig, let me come in.'

And the second little pig answered, 'No, no, not by the hair of my chinny chin chin.'

The wolf replied, 'Then I'll **huff** and I'll **puff**, and I'll blow your house down.'

So he **huffed** and he **puffed**, and he **puffed** and he **huffed**. And, at last, he blew the house down.

The third little pig met a man with a load of bricks. He said to

him, 'Please, mister, give me those bricks so I can build a house.'

The man agreed and the little pig built his house out of bricks.

Then the wolf came along, as he had before, and said, 'Little pig, little pig, let me come in.'

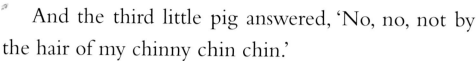

And the third little pig answered, 'No, no, not by the hair of my chinny chin chin.'

The wolf replied, 'Then I'll **huff** and I'll **puff**, and I'll blow your house down.'

Well, he **huffed** and he **puffed**, and he **huffed** and he **puffed**, and he **puffed** and he **huffed**, but he could not blow the house down.

When the wolf found that he couldn't blow the house down, he said, 'Little pig, I know where there's a field full of lovely carrots.'

'Where?' asked the little pig.

'Oh, in Farmer Jones's top field. If you can be ready tomorrow morning, I'll call for you – we'll go there together and get some carrots for dinner.'

'Very well,' said the little pig. 'I'll be ready. What time do you want to go?'

'At six o'clock sharp.'

Well, the little pig was ready at five o'clock in the morning instead, and he went out to pick the carrots before the wolf arrived.

When the wolf arrived an hour later, he said, 'Little pig, it's six o'clock. Are you ready?'

The little pig replied, 'Ready! I've already been to

the field and come back again. I picked a nice bunch of carrots for my dinner.'

The wolf was very angry at this, but he thought that he would catch the little pig out somehow or other, so he said, 'Little pig, I know where there's a nice big apple tree.'

'Where?' asked the little pig.

'Down at Mary's garden,' replied the wolf. 'If you don't trick me, I'll come for you at five o'clock tomorrow morning and we can pick some apples.'

Well, the little pig woke up the next morning at four o'clock and went off to pick the apples, hoping to get back before the wolf arrived. But it was a longer way to go and he had to climb the apple tree. Just as he was climbing down the tree, he saw the wolf arrive, which, as you can imagine, gave him quite a fright.

The wolf said, 'Little pig, so you got here before me. Are they tasty apples?'

'Yes, very,' said the little pig. 'I'll throw you one down.'

He threw the apple so far away that the wolf had to go a long way to pick it up. While he did, the little pig quickly jumped down and was able to run home.

The next day, the wolf came again, and said, 'Little pig, there's a fair at Strawberry Fields this afternoon. Are you going?'

'Oh, yes,' said the little pig, 'I'm going. What time will you be ready?'

'At three o'clock,' said the wolf.

As usual, the little pig set out an hour before the agreed time. He got to the fair, bought a butter churn and was returning home with it when he saw the wolf coming. He didn't know what to do! He hid inside the butter churn and, in doing so, the weight of his body turned it round and round. The butter churn rolled down and down the hill with the little pig inside. This frightened the wolf so much that he ran away without going to the fair.

He went straight to the little pig's house and told him how he had been scared by a great round thing which rolled past him down the hill.

The little pig said, 'Hah! I frightened you, then. I went to the fair and bought a butter churn. When I saw you, I got into it and it rolled down the hill.'

The wolf was very angry indeed, and said, 'I'm going

to climb down the chimney and eat you up.'

When the little pig realised what the wolf was about to do, he hung a pot of water to boil over the fireplace and made up a blazing fire. Just as the wolf was coming down the chimney, the little pig took the lid off the pot, and in fell the wolf. Then the little pig quickly put the lid back on again. He boiled the wolf, and ate him all up for his supper.

Goldilocks
and the
Three Bears

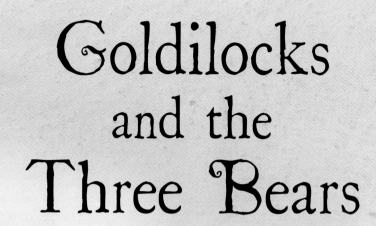

Once upon a time, there was a little girl named Goldilocks. One day, she decided to go for a walk in the forest. She walked a long way and reached a part of the forest she had never been to before. Soon she came to a sweet wooden house.

She was a curious little girl, so she knocked at the door. When no one answered, she walked right in as the door was not locked.

At the table in the kitchen, there were three bowls of porridge. Goldilocks felt very hungry after her walk, so she tasted the porridge from the first bowl.

'This porridge is **too hot**!' she exclaimed.

So she tasted the porridge from the second bowl.

'This porridge is **too cold**,' she said.

So she tasted the last bowl of porridge.

'Ah, this porridge is **just right**,' she said contentedly, and she ate it all up.

After she'd eaten her porridge, she felt a little tired.

She walked into the living room,
where she saw three chairs.

Goldilocks sat on the first chair to
rest her feet.

'This chair is **too big**!' she cried.

So she sat in the second chair.

'This chair is **too big** as well!' she complained.

So she tried the last and smallest chair.

'Ah, this chair is **just right**,' she sighed happily.

But when she sat down
to rest in the chair, she broke
it and it fell to pieces!

Goldilocks was very sleepy by this time, so she went upstairs to the bedroom.

She lay down on the first bed.

'This bed is **too hard**,' she said.

Then she lay down on the second bed.

'This bed is **too soft**,' she complained.

Then she lay down in the third bed.

'Ah, this bed is **just right**,' she cooed.

And Goldilocks was so tired that she soon fell fast asleep.

While she was sleeping, the three bears who lived in the house came back home and went straight to the kitchen to eat their breakfast.

'Someone's been eating my porridge,' growled Daddy Bear.

'Someone's been eating my porridge, too,' said Mummy Bear.

'Someone's been eating my porridge **and they've eaten it all up!**' cried Baby Bear.

Then they all went into the living room.

'Someone's been sitting in my chair,' growled Daddy Bear.

'Someone's been sitting in my chair, too,' said Mummy Bear.

'Someone's been sitting in my chair **and they've broken it all to pieces!**' cried Baby Bear.

The bears decided to look around the house. When they got upstairs to the bedroom, Daddy Bear growled, 'Someone's been sleeping in my bed.'

'Someone's been sleeping in my bed, too,' said Mummy Bear.

'Someone's been sleeping in my bed **and she's still there!**' exclaimed Baby Bear.

Just then, Goldilocks woke up and saw the three bears.

She screamed, 'Help! Help!'

Goldilocks jumped up off the bed and ran out of the room. She dashed down the stairs, opened the door and ran through the forest as fast as she could. Goldilocks was very pleased to get back home in one piece, and she never, ever returned to the house of the three bears.

The Three Billy Goats Gruff

Once upon a time, there were three billy goats. They needed to climb up the hill to eat the juicy, green grass to make themselves fat for the winter. Strangely, although they were different ages, they were all called 'Gruff'.

On the way up the hill, the Billy Goats Gruff had to cross a bridge over a waterfall, and underneath the bridge lived a very ugly troll. His eyes were as big as saucers and he had a huge, bulbous nose.

The youngest Billy Goat Gruff was the first to cross the bridge.

Creak, creak, went the bridge.

'Who's that creeping over my bridge?' growled the troll.

'Oh, it's only me, the youngest Billy Goat Gruff. I'm going up the hill to make myself fat,' said the billy goat in a tiny, little voice.

'**No, you're not. I'm coming to gobble you all up,**' said the troll.

'Oh, no! Please don't. I'm too little,' said the billy goat. 'Wait until the second Billy Goat Gruff comes. He's much bigger than me.'

'**Well, be off with you, then,**' said the troll.

A little while after, the second Billy Goat Gruff started to cross the bridge.

Creak, creak, creak, creak, went the bridge.

'Who's that creeping over my bridge?' roared the troll.

'I'm the second Billy Goat Gruff, and I'm going up the hill to make myself fat,' said the billy goat, who had a louder voice than his younger brother.

'No, you're not. I'm coming to gobble you all up,' said the troll.

'Oh, no! Please don't. Wait until the big Billy Goat Gruff comes. He's much larger than me.'

'Very well! Be off with you, then,' said the troll.

Just then, up came the big Billy Goat Gruff. CREAK, CREAK, CREAK, CREAK, CREAK, CREAK! went the bridge, for the billy goat was so heavy that the bridge could hardly hold him.

'Who's that stomping over my bridge?' grunted the troll.

'It's me, the big Billy Goat Gruff,' said the eldest billy goat, who had a gruff, croaky voice.

'**Now I'm coming to gobble you all up,**' ranted the troll.

'Well, just you try it. I'll poke your eyeballs out and I'll crush your bones to bits,' the big billy goat said.

He ran at the troll, poked his eyes out with his horns, crushed him to bits with his strong legs and tossed him into the waterfall.

Then when the eldest Billy Goat Gruff was finished, he went up the hill and met his two brothers. The three Billy Goats Gruff ate so much grass and grew so fat on the hill that they could hardly walk home again.

Rumpelstiltskin

Once upon a time, there was a poor miller who had a beautiful daughter. He was very proud of his daughter and one day he went to see the king. In order to appear important, he boasted to him, 'I have a daughter who can spin straw into gold.'

The king, who was very fond of money, said to the miller, 'Spinning is something that pleases me very much. If your daughter is as clever as you say, bring her to my palace tomorrow, and I'll put her to the test.'

When the girl was brought to the king, he took her into a room full of straw, gave her a spinning wheel and said, 'Now set to work. If you value your life, you must spin this straw into gold by early tomorrow morning.' Then he locked the room and left her there all alone.

The poor miller's daughter had no idea how straw could be spun into gold, so she began to cry.

All at once the door opened, and in came a little man who said, 'Good evening, young lass. Why are you crying so?'

'Alas,' answered the girl, 'I have to spin straw into gold, and I have no idea how to do it.'

'What will you give me,' asked the dwarf, 'if I do it for you?'

'My necklace,' said the girl.

The little man took the necklace, seated himself in front of the wheel, and whistled and sang, 'Round and round. Round and round. Reel away, reel away. Straw into gold, straw into gold.'

And so it went on until early morning,

when all the straw had been spun
and all the reels were full of gold.

When the king arrived and saw the
gold, he was astonished and delighted,
but he became even greedier. He locked the
miller's daughter into another, larger room full
of straw, and again commanded her to spin it
into gold by early the next morning.

The girl started to wail and then the door
opened and the little man appeared again. He
said, 'What will you give me if I spin that straw
into gold for you?'

'The ring on my finger,' answered the girl.

The little man took the ring, began to turn
the wheel, and whistled and sang, 'Round and
round. Round and round. Reel
away, reel away. Straw into gold,
straw into gold.'

By morning the dwarf had
spun all the straw into gold
once more.

The king was delighted at the sight, but he still didn't have enough gold, so he took the miller's daughter into an even larger room full of straw and said, 'You must spin this during the night. If you succeed, you shall be my queen.'

She's only a miller's daughter, the king thought, *but I'll never find a richer wife in the whole world.*

When the girl was alone in the room, the dwarf visited for the third time and said, 'What will you give me if I spin the straw for you this time?'

'I have nothing left to give you,' answered the girl.

'Then promise me that if you become queen, you'll give me your first child.'

Who knows whether that will ever happen? thought the girl.

Not knowing what else to do, she promised the dwarf what he wanted and he once more spun the straw into gold.

When the king came in the morning and found all the gold he wanted, he married the miller's pretty daughter and she became queen. A year later, her first child was born but she had forgotten all about the dwarf.

However, one day the dwarf came into her room and said, 'Now give me what you promised.'

The queen was horrified and offered him all the riches of the kingdom if only he would leave her the child.

The dwarf replied, 'No, this baby is dearer to me than all the treasures in the world.'

Then the queen began to cry so that the dwarf felt sorry for her.

'I will give you three days,' said he. 'If, by that time, you find out my name, then you can keep your child.'

The queen lay awake that night thinking of all the strange names she had ever heard. She even sent a messenger throughout the kingdom to find out new names.

When the dwarf returned the next day, she began with Ichabod, Melchior, Balthazar and all the other odd names she knew. To every one the little man said, 'No, dear lady, that is not my name.'

On the second day,
she began with all the comical
names she had heard:
'Perhaps your name is Bandy-legs,
Hunchback, Crookshanks . . .'

However, the dwarf always
answered, 'No, madam, that is not my name.'

On the third day the messenger
came back from his travels and said,
'All the time I've been away, I didn't
discover a single new name, but when I
reached the edge of the forest I saw a little
hut. By the hut a fire was burning, and round
the fire was a funny little dwarf, dancing
on one leg, who whistled and sang,
Today I brew, tomorrow bake.
The young queen's child I will take.
Little does the lady dream.
That Rumpelstiltskin is my name.'

The queen danced for joy when she
heard the name.

The little man returned to the queen later that morning and asked, 'Now, your majesty, what is my name?'

At first she asked, 'Is your name Tom?'

'No.'

She paused a little and then asked, 'Is your name Harry?'

'No.'

'Can your name be Rumpelstiltskin?' she asked eventually.

'Some witch told you that! Some witch told you that!' cried the little man.

In his anger he stamped his right foot so hard into the earth that his whole leg went in. He was furious and was forced to take his leg in both his hands to pull himself out. He limped off and nothing more was ever heard from RUMPELSTILTSKIN.

One-Eye, Two-Eyes and Three-Eyes

Once upon a time, there was a woman who had three daughters. The eldest had a single eye in the middle of her forehead and she was called One-Eye. The middle daughter had two eyes like most people and she was called Two-Eyes. But the youngest had three eyes – two on the sides of her head and the third in the middle of her forehead – and she was called Three-Eyes.

The mother loved One-Eye and Three-Eyes very much because they were so different to other girls, but because Two-Eyes was ordinary, her mother and her sisters hated her. They made her life a real misery every way they could. Poor Two-Eyes was treated like a common servant and had to do all the housework. She had only the scraps left on the table to eat and wore ragged old hand-me-down clothes. On top of that, she had to get up very early every morning to tend the small flock of sheep that they owned. One-Eye and Three-Eyes were very lazy and were allowed to sleep in late and do as they wished. They never, ever lifted a finger because Two-Eyes did everything for them.

One day, Two-Eyes went out to the field to look after the sheep. She was so hungry that she burst into tears and was so miserable that she didn't know what to do.

Suddenly, she looked up and saw a mysterious woman standing there.

'Why are you crying, Two-Eyes?' asked the woman.

'I'm very unhappy! My mother and my two sisters hate me because I have two eyes like other people. I wear rags and do all the housework and have nothing but their leftovers to eat. I didn't have any breakfast and I'm starving.'

'Don't cry,' the woman replied. 'Go to that small black lamb over there and whisper in its ear, Bring me a fine table with good things to eat.'

Two-Eyes did as she was told and went up to the little black lamb. As soon as she said the words 'Bring me a fine table with good things to eat', a table appeared, covered in a linen cloth, laid with silver cutlery and with the most scrumptious food on it. There was ham and chicken, tomatoes, lettuce and cucumber, fairy cakes and ice cream, a banana split covered in chocolate sauce – in fact, all of her favourite foods. Two-Eyes was so hungry that she tucked into the feast without stopping once. When she finished eating, the table vanished into thin air.

Two-Eyes returned home and she didn't touch the scraps that her mother gave her.

'I don't want those horrid leftovers,' she cried.

'You ungrateful girl! You'll eat what you're given.' But Two-Eyes refused to eat them.

A few days later, Two-Eyes was still refusing to eat the scraps and her mother became suspicious. She called over One-Eye and said, 'I can't work out why Two-Eyes isn't hungry. Tomorrow when Two-Eyes goes out to tend the sheep, you must follow her and find out what happens.'

The next day, One-Eye, who wasn't used to getting up early, reluctantly followed Two-Eyes to the field where the sheep were kept. However, by lunchtime she was so tired that she fell fast asleep.

When Two-Eyes saw her sister sleeping, she knew it was safe to go up to the little black lamb and say, 'Bring me a fine table with good things to eat.'

One-Eye was sleeping so deeply that she didn't hear these words or see her sister eating at the magic table.

When One-Eye returned home, her mother asked, 'So what happened, then?'

'I don't know. I was so tired walking all that way that I fell asleep.'

The mother turned to Three-Eyes and said, 'Tomorrow you must go and see what happens – and make sure *you* don't fall asleep.'

The next morning, Three-Eyes, who hated getting up at the best of times, followed Two-Eyes to where the sheep were grazing. She too felt very tired and she soon closed her eyes.

When Two-Eyes saw that Three-Eyes was asleep, she whispered to the little lamb, 'Bring me a fine table with good things to eat.'

The magic table appeared again. What she didn't realise was that Three-Eyes wasn't completely asleep. Two of her eyes were sleeping but her middle eye remained awake and could see everything that was happening. She saw Two-Eyes talking to the little black lamb, she saw the magic table appear and Two-Eyes tucking into the wonderful food.

When the table disappeared, Three-Eyes rushed home as fast as her plump little legs could carry her and told her mother about the mystery of the little lamb and the magic table and all the good things on it that Two-Eyes had eaten up so heartily.

The wicked mother was so angry that she went straight out to the little black lamb and killed it with a butcher's knife.

The next morning, Two-Eyes tried to dig a grave for the poor little lamb, but she was so overcome with grief that tears started streaming down her face.

The mystery woman appeared once again and asked, 'Why are you crying?'

'My mother killed the little lamb,' Two-Eyes replied.

'Don't cry,' said the woman. 'Cut out the lamb's heart and bury it outside your window.'

Two-Eyes did as she was told.

The next morning when Two-Eyes woke up, there was a beautiful apple tree outside her bedroom window. It had shiny golden apples and glittering silver leaves. Even though Two-Eyes was still very sad about the poor little lamb, the sight of the wonderful gold and silver tree did cheer her up a bit.

When One-Eye and Three-Eyes and their mother saw the tree, they couldn't stop gaping at it and they were all very puzzled.

'How on earth did that tree get there?' they asked each other.

A handsome young prince happened to be riding by at that moment and when he saw the beautiful golden apple tree he was so amazed that he pulled his horse to a halt.

When the mother saw the prince pull up his horse, she told Two-Eyes to hide herself. 'Get under that bush. You don't want him to see you with your two plain eyes and ragged clothes.'

Two-Eyes went and hid under the shady bush. The prince jumped down from his horse and asked the mother if he could try one of the beautiful golden apples, saying that she could have anything she wished for in return.

The mother curtsied with difficulty and said very politely (which was unusual for her), 'Oh, certainly, your highness, of course. My daughter will pick an apple for you, your highness. Three-Eyes, fetch a ladder, climb up the tree and get an apple for his highness.'

Three-Eyes very clumsily climbed the ladder but when she tried to pick the biggest, juiciest apple, it jumped away from her. Every time she tried, the same thing happened.

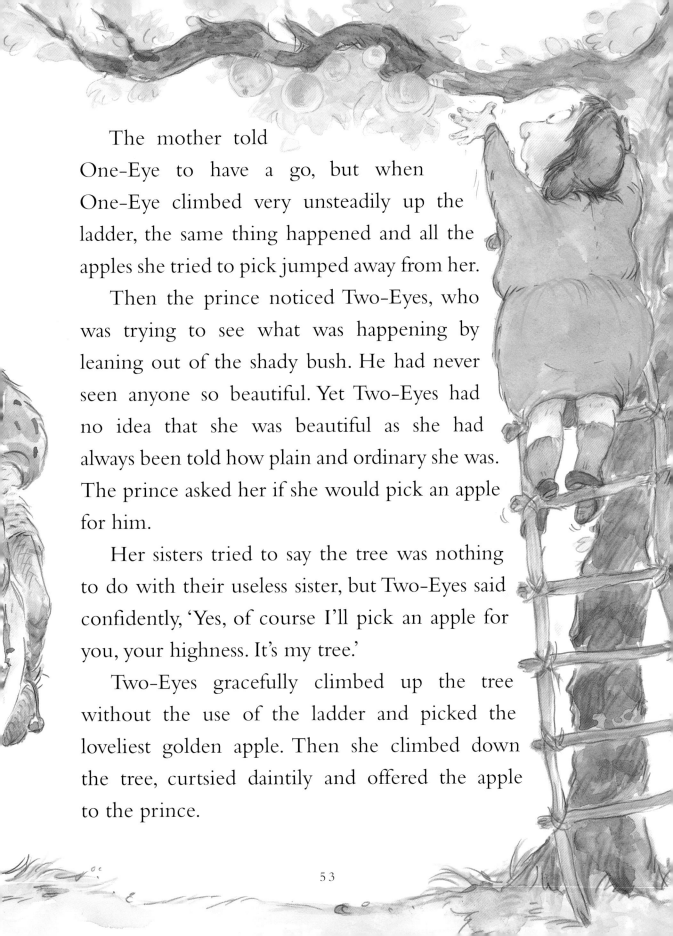

The mother told One-Eye to have a go, but when One-Eye climbed very unsteadily up the ladder, the same thing happened and all the apples she tried to pick jumped away from her.

Then the prince noticed Two-Eyes, who was trying to see what was happening by leaning out of the shady bush. He had never seen anyone so beautiful. Yet Two-Eyes had no idea that she was beautiful as she had always been told how plain and ordinary she was. The prince asked her if she would pick an apple for him.

Her sisters tried to say the tree was nothing to do with their useless sister, but Two-Eyes said confidently, 'Yes, of course I'll pick an apple for you, your highness. It's my tree.'

Two-Eyes gracefully climbed up the tree without the use of the ladder and picked the loveliest golden apple. Then she climbed down the tree, curtsied daintily and offered the apple to the prince.

The prince was enchanted with Two-Eyes and it was love at first sight for both of them. He asked her to marry him and she agreed with delight. They rode off together to his palace and were married immediately.

The next morning when they looked outside their bedroom into the palace gardens, the gold and silver apple tree was growing outside their window.

After Two-Eyes left home, her mother and sisters became increasingly poverty-stricken and had to beg for food. One day, they visited the palace. The mother was truly repentant and regretted how unkind she had been to her middle daughter. One-Eye and Three-Eyes were also ashamed of how badly they had treated their sister. Two-Eyes felt so sorry for them that she forgave them everything. They all hugged each other and they all lived happily ever after in the palace.

The Emperor's New Clothes

Once upon a time, there was an emperor who loved fine new clothes and spent all his money on them. He neglected his people and his army. He had no hobbies and never played any sport. The only reason he left his palace was to be driven around in his open state coach to display his new clothes. He had different robes for every hour of the day.

In his city, strangers were always coming and going, and everyone knew about the emperor's passion for clothes. Two scoundrels who had heard about the vain emperor decided to take advantage of him. They had a cunning plan and introduced themselves at the gates of the palace.

'We're two excellent weavers and we make the most magnificent cloth imaginable. Not only is the material very beautiful but the clothes we make from it have a special power. They're **invisible** to anyone too stupid to see them.'

The chief of the guards heard the scoundrels' odd story and sent for the court chamberlain. The chamberlain notified the prime minister, who rushed to the emperor and told him the news. The emperor was very curious about this material and so he agreed to see the two men.

'Besides being **invisible**, your highness, this cloth will be woven in colours and patterns created especially for you,' they told him.

What a splendid idea, thought the emperor. *What useful clothes for me to have: not only will I have some wonderful new clothes, but I'll also know who is too stupid to work for me.*

The emperor gave the two scoundrels

a bag of gold coins and they promised to begin work on the cloth immediately.

The 'weavers' set up their looms in the emperor's palace. Every day they asked for the finest silk and gold thread to be brought to them but when it arrived they stuffed the thread into their bags. They pretended to work with it at their looms but they produced **nothing**. The looms were empty. They sat at the empty looms late into the night. Night after night they went home with the money the emperor gave them and their bags full of the silk and gold thread. Day after day they pretended to work.

A while later, the emperor was eager to discover how the cloth was looking and wanted to see it for himself. However, he felt rather uneasy.

Maybe, he thought secretly, *I won't be able to see the cloth. That would mean I'm stupid and unfit to be emperor. I can't let that happen.*

He therefore decided to send his faithful old prime minister to check how the weavers were getting on.

He'll be able to see what the cloth looks like – he's far from stupid and is very good at his job, thought the emperor.

So the faithful old prime minister went to the hall where the two weavers sat at the empty looms pretending to work. The emperor's prime minister opened his eyes wide.

Goodness gracious me! he thought. *I see* nothing *at all* – nothing. But he did not say so.

The two villains begged him to come nearer and asked him how he liked the cloth.

'Don't you think that the colours are exquisite? See how intricate the patterns are,' they said.

The poor old prime minister stared and stared. He still couldn't see anything, for there was **nothing** to see. But he did not dare say so.

Nobody must find out, he thought to himself. *I can't confess that I can't see the stuff. I'd be declared unfit to be prime minister.*

'Well,' asked one of the rogues, 'does it please you?'

'Oh, yes, it's excellent – such a beautiful design and such exquisite colours. I'll tell the emperor how wonderful the cloth is.'

'We're very glad to hear that,' said the weavers, gleefully rubbing their hands and describing the colours and patterns in great detail.

The prime minister listened very carefully so that he could repeat everything to the emperor.

The weavers demanded more money and more thread, saying that they needed it to finish the cloth. But, just as before, they put all they were given into their bags and pretended to work at their empty looms.

Soon after this, the emperor sent the court chamberlain to see how the men were getting on and to ask when the cloth would be ready. Exactly the same thing happened with him as with the prime minister. He stood and stared, but as there was **nothing** there, he could see **nothing**.

'Isn't the material beautiful?' asked the scoundrels, and again they mentioned the patterns and the exquisite colours.

I'm certainly not stupid, thought the court chamberlain, *but I must be unfit for my post.*

Nobody must know that I can't see the material.

So the chamberlain praised the material he did not see and said how delighted he was with the colours and marvellous patterns.

When he returned to the emperor, he reported, 'The cloth the weavers are preparing is really magnificent.'

Everybody in the city had heard of the secret cloth and people couldn't stop talking about it. They could hardly wait to see the emperor in his new clothes.

The emperor himself was burning with curiosity to see the cloth which had cost him a small fortune. Accompanied by his ministers, including the prime minister and court chamberlain, the emperor went to the weavers. There they sat in front of the empty looms, weaving extremely hard as usual, but without a single piece of thread.

'Isn't the cloth magnificent, your majesty?' the prime minister asked, even though he couldn't see a thing.

'See here – the splendid pattern and the glorious colours,' said the court chamberlain who had seen **nothing** before and saw **nothing** now.

They both pointed to the empty looms, each thinking that the other could see the material.

What can this mean? thought the emperor. *This is terrible. Am I really so stupid? Am I not fit to be emperor? This is a disaster!*

But aloud the emperor said, 'Oh, the cloth is wonderful. It has a splendid pattern and the colours are charming.' He nodded in approval and smiled at the empty looms. He would not, could not admit that he saw **nothing** when his two ministers had praised the material so highly.

All the emperor's men stared and stared at the empty looms. Not one of them saw **anything** there, but they all said, 'Oh, the cloth is magnificent!'

They suggested that the emperor should have a new suit made from this splendid material to wear in a great procession the following day, so that all his people could see his fine new clothes.

Everyone present muttered,

'Yes, yes! Excellent! Splendid idea!' Even though nobody could see **anything** at all.

Again the rogues sat up all night and pretended to work (burning at least twenty candles in the process), so that everyone could see how busy they were making the suit of clothes in time for the procession. Each weaver had a great big pair of scissors that they cut into the air, pretending to cut the cloth with them, and sewing with no thread in their needles.

Everyone in the palace was excited and the emperor's clothes were the talk of the town. At last, the weavers declared that the clothes were ready and the emperor and his entire court came to the weavers. Each of the scoundrels lifted up an arm as if he were holding something.

'Here are your majesty's trousers,' said one.

'This is your majesty's train,' said the other.

'The whole suit is as light as a spider's web,' said the first. 'Why, you almost feel as if you have nothing on – and that's the beauty of it.' At this stage they were finding it hard to keep straight faces.

'Magnificent,' cried the ministers, even

though they could see **nothing** at all.

'Now if your majesty would kindly take off your clothes,' said the weavers, 'we'll fit you with the new ones.'

So the emperor took off his clothes down to his underpants, and the scoundrels pretended to help him, garment by garment, into the new clothes they had pretended to make.

The emperor turned from side to side in front of the long glass, pretending to admire himself.

'How well they fit. How splendid your majesty's robes look. What gorgeous colours!' everyone said.

'The procession is waiting, your majesty,' announced the prime minister.

'I'm quite ready,' announced the emperor.

The courtiers who had to carry the emperor's train felt about on the ground and pretended to lift it. They walked solemnly behind the emperor, pretending to carry the train. Nobody would admit that they couldn't see the clothes, for fear of being thought stupid or unfit for their posts.

All the people standing in the streets and at the windows cheered and cried, 'Oh, the emperor's new clothes are splendid. What a magnificent train! How well the clothes fit!'

No one dared to admit that he couldn't see **anything**, for who wanted to be thought stupid? None of the emperor's clothes had ever met with such success.

However, from among the crowds a little boy suddenly cried out, 'But he's not wearing **any clothes**. He hasn't got **anything** on.'

Everyone began to whisper to each other and repeat what the boy had said: 'He hasn't got **anything** on! A little boy is saying he hasn't got **anything** on!'

And then the whole city was saying, 'But he hasn't got **anything** on.'

Soon the emperor heard what they were whispering and he knew it was true – all he had on were his baggy underpants. *But I'll have to go through with this procession, come what may*, he thought.

So he drew himself up tall and walked boldly on, holding his head higher than before, and the courtiers pretended to carry the train that **wasn't there at all**.

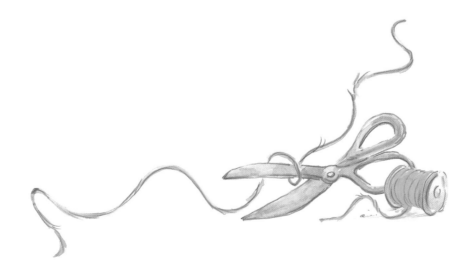

Jack and the Beanstalk

Once upon a time, there was a poor widow who had one son named Jack, and a cow named Milk-White. All they had to live on was the milk the cow gave them each morning. Every morning they carried the milk to the market and sold it. But one morning Milk-White stopped giving milk and they didn't know what to do.

'What shall we do, what

shall we do?' said the widow, wringing her hands.

'Cheer up, Mother. I'll go and get work somewhere,' said Jack, an eternal optimist.

'Who would take on a young boy like you?' asked his mother. 'No, we must sell Milk-White and with the money we'll start a shop or something.'

'All right, Mother,' said Jack. 'I'll soon sell Milk-White and then we'll see what we can do.'

So Jack took the cow's harness in his hand, and off he set.

He hadn't gone very far when he met a funny-looking old man who said to him, 'Good morning, Jack.'

'Good morning to you,' said Jack, wondering how the old man knew his name.

'Well, Jack, where are you off to?' asked the man.

'I'm going to market to sell our cow here.'

'Oh, well, good luck to you, then,' said the man. 'But let me ask you a question first: do you know how many beans make five?'

'Two in each hand and one in your mouth,' said Jack very sharply.

'Right you are,' said the man, 'and here are the very beans themselves.' From out of his pocket he pulled five strange-looking beans. 'As you're so sharp, I don't mind doing a swap with you: your cow here for these beans.'

'Why would I want to do that?' asked Jack. 'It doesn't seem like a fair exchange to me.'

'Ah! You don't know what these beans are,' said the man. 'If you plant them overnight, by morning they will grow right up to the sky.'

'Really?' exclaimed Jack in disbelief. 'You don't say.'

'Yes, that's so, and if it doesn't turn out to be true you can have your cow back.'

'OK,' said Jack, and he handed over Milk-White to the old man and put the five beans in his pocket.

Jack went back home, and as he hadn't gone to the market it was still quite early by the time he returned.

'What, back already, Jack?' said his mother. 'I see you haven't got Milk-White with you, so you've sold her already, have you? How much did you get for her, then?'

'You'll never guess, Mother,' said Jack.

'No, I can't. Five pounds, ten, fifteen . . . surely it can't be twenty?'

'I said you couldn't guess! Look at these beans! They're magical – plant them overnight and –'

'What?' said Jack's mother. 'What a fool, what an idiot, what an imbecile, to give away my Milky-White! She's the best giver of milk for miles around, and all you get for her are some paltry beans?' She was so annoyed that she boxed Jack's ears. 'And as for your precious beans – they're worthless.'

She grabbed hold of the beans and threw them out of the window.

'Now off to bed with you. There's no food and no drink for you tonight, you stupid boy.'

The poor mother was beside herself and collapsed in a heap on the floor, her head in her hands.

Jack went upstairs to his little room in the attic, and very sad and sorry he was too. He couldn't stop fretting about what he had done and he was also extremely hungry.

At last, after tossing and turning, he dropped off to sleep. When he woke up, the room was strangely dark. Jack jumped out of bed and went to the window. And you'll never guess what he saw! The beans his mother had thrown out of the window into the garden had sprung up into a big beanstalk which went up and up and up to the sky.

So the man was telling the truth after all, thought Jack.

The beanstalk was growing up past Jack's window, and he just opened the window and jumped on to the beanstalk, which looked like a big plaited ladder.

Jack was so curious to

discover where it went that he climbed and he climbed and he climbed and he climbed and he climbed, until at last he reached the sky. When he reached the top he found a long, straight road stretching into the distance. So he walked and he walked and he walked along the road, until he came to a great big tall house, where there was a great big tall woman on the doorstep.

'Good morning, madam,' said Jack very politely. 'Would you be so kind as to give me some breakfast please?' He was starving as he hadn't had anything to eat for such a long time.

'You want some breakfast, do you?' said the great big tall woman. 'You'll *be* breakfast if you don't push off. My husband is an ogre and there's nothing he likes better than boys on toast for his breakfast! You'd better be moving on as he'll be coming back soon.'

'Oh, please, madam, do give me something to eat. I've had nothing to eat since yesterday morning,' said Jack. 'I'm so hungry I may as well be eaten for breakfast for I'll die of hunger soon.'

Well, the ogre's wife wasn't such a mean person after all and she took Jack into the kitchen. She gave him a hunk of bread and cheese and a jug of milk. Jack was wolfing it all down but before he could finish, he heard, **Thump! Thump! Thump!** The whole house began to tremble with the noise of someone coming closer.

'Oh dear! It's my old man,' said the ogre's wife. 'Quick! Jump in here.' She bundled Jack into the oven just as the ogre came through the door.

He was the most enormous giant in the whole world. He had three sheep tied by their heels to his belt. He unhooked them, threw them down on the table and said, 'Here, wife, cook me these sheep for breakfast. Ah, ah, and what's this I smell? **Fee-fi-fo-fum**, I smell the blood of an Englishman! Be he alive, or be he dead, I'll grind his bones to make my bread.'

'Nonsense, dear,' said his wife. 'You're dreaming. Or perhaps you can still smell the leftovers of that little boy you had for dinner yesterday. Go and have a wash and tidy up, and by the time you come back, your breakfast will be ready for you.'

So off the ogre went and Jack was just about to jump out of the oven and run off, when the woman said, 'No, wait until he's asleep. He always has a snooze after breakfast.'

The ogre ate his breakfast and then he went to a big chest. He opened the lid and took out two bags of gold. Then he sat down at the table and started counting the gold pieces, until at last his head began to nod. He started to snore and the whole house shook again.

Jack crept out on tiptoe from the oven. As he went past the ogre he put one of the bags of gold under his arm, and ran off as fast as he could. When he reached the beanstalk he threw down the bag of gold, which fell straight into his mother's garden. Then he climbed down and down and down, until at last he arrived home.

He showed his mother the gold and said, 'Well, Mother, wasn't I right about the beans? They really are magical!'

They lived on the bag of gold for some time but at last they came to the end of it, so Jack made up his mind to try his luck at the top of the beanstalk once more.

On the next fine morning, he got up early, climbed out of his window and on to the beanstalk. He climbed and climbed and climbed and climbed and climbed, until at last he arrived at the road again and reached the great big tall house as before. There, as before, was the great big tall woman standing on the doorstep.

'Good morning, madam,' said Jack, as bold as you like. 'Could you please be so kind as to give me something to eat?'

'Go away, boy,' said the great big tall woman, 'or else my man will eat you up for breakfast. Hey! Aren't you the little chap who came here once before? Do you know, that very same day my man found one of his bags of gold missing?'

'That's strange, madam,' said Jack. 'Maybe I can tell you something about that, but I'm so hungry I won't be able to speak until I've had something to eat.'

Well, the great big tall woman was so curious that she took Jack in and gave him something to eat. But he had hardly started eating when he heard, Thump! Thump! Thump! It was the sound of the giant's footsteps, so his wife hid Jack away in the oven again and the same thing happened as before.

In came the ogre and he said, 'Fee-fi-fo-fum, I smell the blood of an Englishman! Be he alive, or be he dead, I'll grind his bones to make my bread.'

His wife made him a breakfast of three roasted pigs. After he had polished off the lot, he said, 'Wife, bring me the hen that lays the golden eggs.'

So she brought the hen and the ogre said, 'Lay.'

And the hen laid an egg of pure gold. But the ogre was very sleepy and he began to nod his head and his snores shook the house.

Then Jack crept out of the oven on tiptoe. He grabbed hold of the golden hen and was off like a streak of lightning. But the hen clucked and the ogre woke up and just as Jack left the house he heard him calling, 'Wife, wife, what have you done with my golden hen?'

And the wife said, 'Why, my dear?'

But that was all Jack heard, for he rushed off to the beanstalk and climbed down as fast as a rocket. When he got home, he showed his mother the wonderful hen and said, 'Lay.' Every time he said this, the hen laid a golden egg.

His mother was quite satisfied with the wonderful hen, but Jack was not and it wasn't very long before he decided to have another try of his luck at the top of the beanstalk.

One fine morning, he rose early and got on to the beanstalk, and he climbed and he climbed and he climbed and he climbed and he climbed, until he reached the top. But this time he knew better than to go straight to the ogre's house, and he waited behind a bush until he saw the ogre's wife come out with a bucket to fetch some water. Then he crept inside and got into the copper for boiling water.

He hadn't been there long when, as before, he heard, **Thump! Thump! Thump!** Both the ogre and his wife came in.

'**Fee-fi-fo-fum**, I smell the blood of an **Englishman! Be he alive, or be he dead, I'll grind his bones to make my bread**,' the ogre cried out. 'I smell him, wife, I smell him!'

'Are you sure, my dear?' said the ogre's wife. 'If it's that little rogue who stole your gold and the hen, I bet he's in the oven.'

So they both rushed to the oven. But Jack wasn't there and the ogre's wife said, 'What's this with your **fee-fi-fo-fum**? It must be the smell of that lad you caught last night and who I cooked for your late supper. Your problem is, you can't tell the difference between a live one and a dead one.'

The ogre sat down to his breakfast of five-goat-stew. Every now and then he would mutter, 'Well, I could have sworn . . .' And he would get up and search the larder, the cupboards and everywhere, but – luckily – not the copper boiler.

After breakfast, the ogre called out, 'Wife, wife, bring me my golden harp.'

She brought the harp and put it on the table before him.

Then he said, 'Sing!'

The golden harp sang the most beautiful tunes. And it went on singing until the ogre fell asleep and started to snore like thunder.

Then Jack lifted up the copper boiler's lid very carefully and crept down from it as quiet as a mouse on his hands and knees until he reached the table. He got up on to the table top and caught hold of the golden harp and dashed towards the door with it.

But the harp called out loudly, 'Master! Master!'

The ogre woke up just in time to see Jack running off with his harp.

Jack ran as fast as he could, and the ogre came

rushing out and would soon have caught up with him but Jack managed to dodge him, zigzagging down the road. He reached the beanstalk and the ogre was no more than twenty paces away when he saw Jack suddenly disappear. When the ogre came to the end of the road, Jack was underneath him and climbing down the beanstalk as fast as he could.

The ogre didn't trust the beanstalk to hold his huge bulk, so he stood and waited, but then the harp cried out, 'Master! Master!'

The ogre swung himself down on to the beanstalk, which shook with his tremendous weight.

Down and down and down climbed Jack, and after him climbed the ogre. But Jack was very nearly home, so he called out, 'Mother! Mother! Bring me an axe, bring me an axe.'

And his mother came rushing out of the cottage with the axe in her hand, but when she reached the beanstalk she was paralysed with fright for she saw the ogre coming down from the clouds.

Jack jumped off the beanstalk, grabbed the axe and chopped and chopped at the beanstalk until it was nearly cut in two. The ogre felt the beanstalk shake and quiver so he stopped to see what was wrong. Jack gave another chop with the axe and the beanstalk began to topple over. The ogre fell down and hit his head and the beanstalk came toppling down after him.

Jack showed his mother the golden harp which sang the most beautiful tunes. They sold the harp but they kept the hen so they could continue to sell the golden eggs. Jack and his mother became very rich and, of course, they lived happily ever after.

The Ugly Duckling

It was a beautiful summer. The wheat swaying in the light breeze was bright yellow, the oats were a deep green and all the hay had already been made into haystacks. Near the farm meadows was a thick wood, and in the middle of the wood was a lovely, glistening lake.

In a secluded part of the lake where the reeds had grown very tall, a duck had chosen to make her nest. She had been sitting on her eggs for quite a while now, and if the truth be told, she was getting rather bored with all the waiting. She missed the other ducks that were swimming about on other parts of the lake.

At last, the eggs started to crack, and one little head after another appeared.

'Quack, quack,' said the duck to all her children.

The ducklings peeped out from under the reeds, curious to see their new world. It was all so different when they had been inside the eggshells.

'How big everything is,' said one.

'This lake is just a small part of the world – the world goes on for ever and ever. Now, are you all here?' The mother duck started counting them. 'One, two, three, four, five, six . . . Oh, no, they aren't all hatched yet – the largest egg is still here! That's odd because I thought there were only six eggs. Oh dear, how long will this last? I'm so tired!' She sat down again on the largest egg to keep it warm.

That day one of her old friends paid her an unexpected visit.

'How are you getting on, then?' she asked.

'This one egg just won't break. But look at the others – they're the prettiest little ducklings I've ever seen. Not like their father, the good-for-nothing old rogue – he hasn't been to visit me once.'

'Let's see if that egg will break now,' said the old duck. She craned her neck into the nest and had a good look. 'Well, blow me down, that's a turkey's egg! Leave it be and go and teach the ducklings to swim.'

'I'll sit on it a while longer,' said the mother duck. 'I've been sitting so long I may as well just carry on.'

'Well, it's no business of mine.' And away the old duck waddled in a huff.

The great egg burst at last.

'Cheep, cheep,' it said, as it tumbled out of the eggshell.

Oh, but how large and ugly it is, thought the mother. *It's nothing like the others. It's a huge, strong thing! Could it really be a young turkey, like my old friend suggested?*

The next day in the warm sunshine, the mother duck pushed the strange duckling into the water to see if it would swim or not.

And lo and behold, it did.

Soon she and her young family could be seen on the water. They swam in a perfect way, all in a line, their legs moving without any effort. They were all there, even the ugly grey one.

It can't be a turkey after all, thought the mother duck. *See how well it moves its legs and how straight its neck is. He's not so very ugly if you look at him properly.*

'Quack, quack! Follow me now, children, I'll take you back to the farmyard, but you must keep close to me or you may be trodden on. Above all, beware of the cat.'

When they reached the farmyard, a huge argument could be heard: two ducks were squabbling over an eel, and then after all their fighting it was carried off by the cat.

'See, children, that is the way of the world,' said the mother duck. 'Come on, don't turn your toes!

Spread your feet wide apart, bend your necks and say "quack".'

The ducklings did as they were told, but the other farmyard ducks stared and said, 'Look – more ducks, humph! As if there aren't enough of us here already! And what a strange-looking bird one of them is – we don't want him here!'

One duck even flew over the poor ugly duckling and bit him in the neck.

'Leave him alone,' said the mother. 'He's not doing anyone any harm.'

'But he's so big and ugly,' said the spiteful duck. 'He should be thrown out.'

The mother duck stroked the ugly duckling's neck and smoothed his feathers, saying to no one in particular, 'I think he'll grow up strong and able to take care of himself.'

The family of ducks made themselves comfortable in the farmyard. However, the ugly duckling was bitten and pushed around and made fun of, not only by the ducks, but by all the farmyard birds, especially the turkeys.

'He's too big and ugly,' everybody said.

The ugly duckling was quite miserable in the farmyard. The poor thing was bullied by everyone. The girl who fed the birds kicked him. Even his brothers and sisters were unkind, saying, 'You're so ugly. I wish the cat would catch you.'

After a week of this he decided he'd had enough and ran away, flying over the farmyard fence. He flew to a large moor where wild ducks lived. He stayed there for the night, feeling very tired and sorry for himself.

In the morning, the wild ducks stared at him. 'What sort of a duck are you?' they all asked, surrounding him.

He could not reply to their question.

'You're very ugly,' said the wild ducks, 'so keep well away from us.'

After he had been on the moor a few days, two wild geese arrived. Soon there was the sound of gunshots, with men shouting and dogs barking.

BANG, BANG! went the guns and the two wild geese fell dead among the rushes. Blue smoke from the guns rose over the dark trees and a pack of hunting dogs bounded into the rushes. A large vicious dog appeared beside the duckling. His jaws were open, his tongue hung from his mouth and his red eyes were glaring. The poor duckling was terrified! He turned his head around to hide it under his wing. The dog pushed his nose close to the duckling, baring his sharp teeth, and then, all of a sudden, he dived into the water without touching him.

Oh, sighed the duckling with relief, *it's lucky I'm so ugly – even a dog won't bite me.*

He lay quite still in the rushes until he could no longer hear the sound of gunfire. Then he waited a while longer. Finally, he flew through a stormy sky over fields and meadows, and towards evening he reached a little cottage with its door open. He sought shelter inside the cottage and lay down. He was exhausted and a bad storm was getting up.

An old woman, a tomcat and a hen lived in this cottage. The tomcat was a great favourite with his mistress; he had a very loud purr and could throw out sparks from his fur if it was stroked the wrong way. The hen laid good eggs and the woman was very fond of her, too.

In the morning, they saw their strange visitor and the tomcat began to purr and the hen began to cluck.

'What's that noise all about?' demanded the old woman.

She looked around the room but her sight

wasn't very good. When she saw the ugly duckling she thought it must be a fat duck that had strayed from home.

'Oh, what a prize! Hopefully I'll get some duck's eggs from it, but I must wait and see. It could be a male duck – I mean, a *drake* – who can't lay any eggs!'

The duckling was allowed to stay in the cottage for three weeks but in that time he never laid an egg. The hen and the tomcat looked down on the duckling and every time he tried to speak, they wouldn't let him say a word.

'Can you lay eggs?' asked the hen.

'No,' replied the duckling.

'Then hold your tongue.'

'Can you purr or throw out sparks?' asked the tomcat.

'No.'

'Then keep quiet.'

So the duckling sat in a corner, downhearted and not daring to say a word. Through the open doorway, he could feel the sunshine and fresh air beyond, and he had such a great longing to swim on the water that he just had to tell the hen.

'How absurd,' said the hen. 'It's because you're so idle. If you could purr or lay eggs, you wouldn't have these urges.'

'But it's so lovely swimming on the water,' said the duckling, 'especially when you dive down to the bottom.'

'You must be crazy! Who else but you would like to swim in water or dive down to the bottom? Certainly not my mistress, and neither the tomcat nor me, indeed!'

'You don't understand me,' said the duckling sadly.

'We don't understand you? Who do you think you are? Do you think yourself cleverer than me or the tomcat or the old woman? For your own good, I advise you to lay eggs and learn to purr as quickly as possible.'

'I think it's time to go out into the world again,' decided the duckling.

'Yes, you do that,' said the hen.

So the duckling left the cottage and soon found some water where he could swim and dive. However, all the other animals still avoided him because he was so ugly.

Autumn came and the leaves in the forest turned to orange and gold. As winter approached, the leaves fell off the trees and there was snow in the air. This made the poor little duckling very wretched.

One evening, just as the sun was setting, a large flock of beautiful birds flew overhead. The duckling had never seen anything like them before. They were swans with tall, graceful necks, orange beaks and soft, white feathers. There was also a pair of black swans with them, who were slightly smaller and had red beaks. As they flew higher and higher in the sky, they let out a peculiar cry and the ugly duckling felt quite strange. He turned himself around in the water, stretched out his neck towards them and uttered a cry so similar to theirs that he frightened himself.

How beautiful they are, he thought.

He would never forget those lovely, graceful birds. When at last they disappeared, he dived under the water and rose straight up again, feeling very excited. He didn't know the names of these birds nor where they had flown to, but he felt very close to them and he had never had feelings like this before.

If only I was as lovely as them, he sighed.

The winter grew colder and colder and the poor duckling had to swim about on the water to keep it from freezing over. Every night the space where he swam became smaller and smaller and the water was nearly all covered in ice. He had to furiously paddle with his legs to keep a little space free from ice. On the coldest night, he became

exhausted and lay, still and helpless, frozen fast in the ice.

Early next morning, a farmer passing by discovered the poor bird. He broke the ice with his boot and carried him home to his wife. He stayed with them for the rest of the winter. Even though the farmer's children terrified him at least he was warm at the farmer's house.

When spring finally arrived, he felt the warm sunshine on his feathers and he felt strong as he flapped his wings against his sides and rose into the air. He kept flying and soon found himself by a large pond in a country garden, where the cherry trees were in full blossom and tulips and irises were growing in the grass. Everything looked fresh and bright in the early spring sunlight. Then three beautiful white swans arrived, rustling their feathers and swimming lightly over the smooth water. The duckling remembered the lovely birds and felt unhappier than ever.

They'll attack me because I'm so ugly, he thought, *but I just don't care what happens to me any more. I've suffered long enough.*

Then he flew on to the water and swam towards the beautiful swans. They rushed to meet him with outstretched wings. He thought they wanted to kill him and he bent his head down to the surface of the water. But then he saw his own image reflected in the pond – he was no longer a dark grey, ugly bird but a graceful and beautiful swan! He didn't mind how many terrible things he had endured in the past because now he was filled with **happiness**. The swans swam round him and stroked his neck with their beaks, welcoming him into their flock.

Some little children came into the garden and threw bread and cake into the water.

'See,' cried one, 'there's a new swan!'

'The new one is the most beautiful of all – he's so young and pretty!' said another.

The young swan was shy and hid his head under

his wing. He was so happy he didn't know what to do with himself.

I'm a swan, a beautiful swan. I'm not an ugly duckling at all!